On the Road

Timothy's
Five-City Tour

Written by Gare Thompson
Illustrated by Ken Bowser

STECK-VAUGHN
ELEMENTARY · SECONDARY · ADULT · LIBRARY

A Harcourt Classroom Education Company

www.steck-vaughn.com

Contents

Timothy was excited. He was going on his first trip with his school band. They would play in five cities. The last stop would be the White House!

"Be good and listen to Mr. Mask," said Timothy's mother and father. They waved good-bye.

"Everything will be fine," called Timothy. "I'll write to you." Timothy waved good-bye. They were off.

June 29

Dear Mom and Dad,
  Everything is fine on the road. Well, except our bus got a flat tire. Then Sophia lost one of her two drum sticks during drum practice. She kept missing the beat. Otto crawled on the floor to find the drum stick. Mr. Mask was mad about it all. But I'm having fun.

Love, Timothy

P.S. On the bus, we sang the same song one thousand times!

June 30

Dear Mom and Dad,
    Everything is fine. We stayed in a nice hotel last night. Roger, Otto, and I ate and ate all night long. We didn't even have to pay for all the food we ate. We just signed a paper each time. That was great! I can't wait to get to Boston tomorrow!

Love, Timothy

P.S. Mr. Mask fainted when he paid the hotel bill this morning. I wonder if he's sick.

July 1

Dear Mom and Dad,

Everything is fine in Boston today. We played a concert in the park, but our music kept blowing away. Then we went to the John Hancock Tower building. It's very tall and all glass. Sophia kept looking at herself in the windows. Otto got stuck in the elevator. He yelled all the way to the top floor and back! I'm having fun.

Love, Timothy

P.S. Mr. Mask is looking tired.

July 2

Dear Mom and Dad,
    We're still in Boston. Today we saw the ocean and a famous ship. A long time ago, some people threw some tea off the ship into the water. I didn't know why it was important, but the ship was fun anyway. Roger bumped Otto into the water. Otto raced with some fish and chased them away. We had fun!

                                        Love, Timothy

P.S. Mr. Mask looks worse today.

Dear Mom and Dad,   July 3

We went from Boston to New York City today. We had lunch on the bus, but it was messy. Roger dropped his cheese on Sophia. She moved too fast and hit me.. I jumped and spilled ice water all over Mr. Mask. The floor was wet. It was a great bus ride!

                                        Love, Timothy

P.S. Mr. Mask said that we could not eat or drink anything on the bus anymore.

July 4

Dear Mom and Dad,

Everything is fine. Today we were in a Fourth of July parade in New York City. Otto broke his clarinet, so he could only make squeaking noises. It was funny, but Mr. Mask didn't laugh. He held his ears while he marched. Then he fell into a big water puddle.

Love, Timothy

P.S. On the bus ride back to the hotel, we sang the peanut butter song some more.

9

July 5

Dear Mom and Dad,

Everything is fine. Today we went to the top of the Empire State Building. Otto got stuck in the elevator again, so the rest of us walked up the stairs. I asked if anyone had ever dropped water balloons from the top of the building. Mr. Mask said, "Don't even think of doing it." After that, we walked back to our hotel. I'm having fun.

Love, Timothy

P.S. Why is Mr. Mask losing his hair?

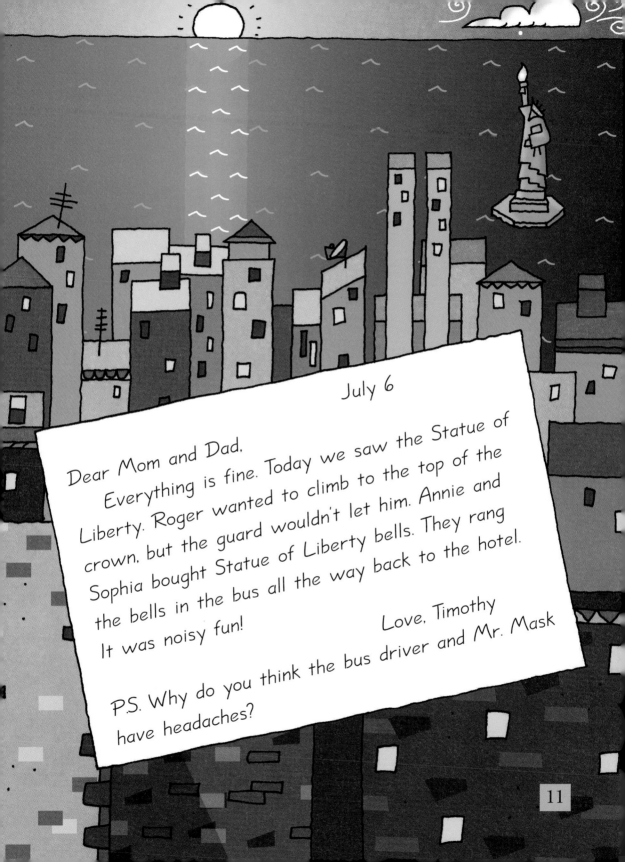

July 6

Dear Mom and Dad,

Everything is fine. Today we saw the Statue of Liberty. Roger wanted to climb to the top of the crown, but the guard wouldn't let him. Annie and Sophia bought Statue of Liberty bells. They rang the bells in the bus all the way back to the hotel. It was noisy fun!

Love, Timothy and Mr. Mask

P.S. Why do you think the bus driver and Mr. Mask have headaches?

Dear Mom and Dad,   July 7
    We're off to Philadelphia. Oh, the bus driver
quit. He said he couldn't take any more. Then he
bought us train tickets. That was nice. On the train,
Roger saw a red cord and pulled it. He just wanted
to see what it was for. The train stopped
REALLY fast!

                                    Love, Timothy
P.S. Pretzels can fly really far when a train stops
quickly.

July 8

Dear Mom and Dad,
    Philadelphia is great. We played a concert in a park today. We're starting to sound a little better as a band. There were some horses pulling carriages around the park. Mr. Mask put us all in a carriage for a ride. Mr. Mask really liked it. He smiled when Otto and Roger fell asleep. At least he knew where we were.

Love, Timothy

P.S. Why did Mr. Mask like the ride?

Philadelphia
July 8

DO NOT TOUCH

Dear Mom and Dad,   July 9

We saw the Liberty Bell this morning. It has a big crack in it. Mr. Mask probably thinks that we did that. The guard said that we could not ring the bell. Why do they keep a bell that won't ring? We bought little liberty bells in the gift shop and rang them all day. It was fun.

Love, Timothy

P.S. Mr. Mask says his ears are ringing.

July 10

Dear Mom and Dad,

Day three in Philadelphia. Today we went to see Ben Franklin's house. He is famous for flying a kite. Why is that a big deal? I've flown a kite lots of times, and no one has written a story about me. The tour guide frowned when I asked. We didn't stay long after that. Mr. Mask told me to stop asking questions.

Love, Timothy

P.S. I think Mr. Mask is pulling out his hair.

July 11

Dear Mom and Dad,

Everything is fine. We're on the train to Baltimore. The train conductor stayed with us to make sure nobody pulled the red cord again. Mr. Mask fell asleep. We rang our bells and sang. Other people on our train car moved to a different car. I wonder why.

Love, Timothy

P.S. Mr. Mask said he wished he could go to another train car, too.

July 12

Baltimore

July 12

Dear Mom and Dad,

We're in Baltimore now. It's on a bay where huge ships come in from the ocean. We ate at an outdoor market. Otto jumped in the water and swam with some crabs. They raced and he won.

Love, Timothy

P.S. Mr. Mask got really cold when he had to jump in the water to get Otto.

Dear Mom and Dad,

July 13

We went to the Babe Ruth House in Baltimore today. A famous baseball player was born there. Seeing the old baseball stuff was cool. Mr. Mask kept saying, "Don't touch anything." Then we went to a city park and played a concert. We were pretty good.

Love, Timothy

P.S. Why weren't there candy bars at the Babe Ruth House?

BAT

GLOVE

BABE

July 14

Dear Mom and Dad,
    Today we went to Fort McHenry. It is on some land that sticks out in Baltimore Harbor. Annie, Sophia, Roger, and I had our pictures taken next to an old cannon. We tried to put a cannonball in the cannon, but Mr. Mask made us stop. The fort was fun!

                    Love, Timothy

P.S. I wonder why Mr. Mask worries so much.

Dear Mom and Dad,   July 15

We're on a new bus on our way to Washington, D.C. Mr. Mask said this would be a short bus ride. He asked us not to sing the peanut butter song again. So we sang the row your boat song one hundred times. The new bus driver didn't sing along. It was fun.

Love, Timothy

P.S. Mr. Mask pulled more hair out. Why is he doing that?

July 16

Washington, D.C.
July 16

Dear Mom and Dad,

We rode on a tour bus today. The first stop was at the Washington Monument. It's white and very tall. It's the tallest building in the city. There's an elevator in the monument, but we wanted to climb the 500 stairs. Otto tried to help some people off the bus, but he slipped. Then the people piled up after him. I had fun.

Love, Timothy

P.S. The bus driver told us not to hurry back.

July 17

Dear Mom and Dad,
    Today we went to the White House. That's where the President lives. We saw the Lincoln room, but Abraham Lincoln wasn't there. Did you know they won't let anyone jump on his bed? We played a concert after we saw the house. It was pretty good. Even Mr. Mask said so.
                                              Love, Timothy

P.S. The President really likes band music!

July 17

Dear Mom and Dad,

We're still at the White House. We would have left earlier, but Otto opened a door and set off an alarm. Annie tried to use a special red telephone and set off another alarm. There were guards everywhere! They had to check everyone.

Love, Timothy

P.S. We got to ride away from The White House in a big, black car. Mr. Mask said he may quit soon.

Dear Mom and Dad,   July 18

    Today the big, black car took us near the
President's private jet. We were just going to look
inside it, but Roger hit a button and we took off.
The pilot said he'd bring us home, so we are on
the way. I think he wants to get rid of us.
Anyway, I'll be home soon!

                                                    Love, Timothy

    P.S. Can I go on the band trip again next year?